Ex Libris

Over the River and

THE NEW ENGLAND BOY'S SONG

L. Maria Child

Through the Wood

ABOUT THANKSGIVING DAY

ILLUSTRATED BY Matt Tavares

CANDLEWICK PRESS

Over the river, and through the wood,

To grandfather's house we go;

The horse knows the way,

To carry the sleigh,

Through the white and drifted snow.

Over the river, and through the wood,

To grandfather's house away!

We would not stop

For doll or top,

For it is Thanksgiving day.

Over the river, and through the wood,

Oh, how the wind does blow!

It stings the toes,

And bites the nose,

As over the ground we go.

Over the river, and through the wood,

With a clear blue winter sky,

The dogs do bark,

And children hark,

As we go jingling by.

Over the river, and through the wood,
To have a first-rate play —

Hear the bells ring
Ting a ling ding,
Hurra for Thanksgiving day!

Over the river, and through the wood,

No matter for winds that blow

Or if we get

The sleigh upset,

Into a bank of snow.

Over the river, and through the wood,

To see little John and Ann;

We will kiss them all,

And play snow-ball,

And stay as long as we can.

Over the river, and through the wood,

Trot fast, my dapple grey!

Spring over the ground,

Like a hunting hound,

For 't is Thanksgiving day!

Over the river, and through the wood,

And straight through the barn-yard gate;

We seem to go

Extremely slow,

It is so hard to wait.

Over the river, and through the wood —

Old Jowler hears our bells;

He shakes his pow,

With a loud bow wow,

And thus the news he tells.

Over the river, and through the wood,

When grandmother sees us come

She will say, Oh dear,

The children are here,

Bring a pie for every one.

Over the river, and through the wood,

Now grandmother's cap I spy!

Hurra for the fun!

Is the pudding done?

Hurra for the pumpkin pie!

A Note about the Author

~~~~~

LYDIA MARIA CHILD was born Lydia Francis in 1802 in Medford, Massachusetts, a town outside Boston. She was the youngest of seven children and moved to Maine to live with her older sister after their mother died. It was there that she studied to become a teacher and began writing. In 1824, she published her first novel, *Hobomok: A Tale of Early Times*. She continued to publish books and also became the editor of the first American children's magazine, the *Juvenile Miscellany*.

In 1828, Lydia Maria married David Child. She was active in many important social movements of her time and wrote often about abolishing slavery, allowing women to vote, and upholding the rights of Native Americans.

Lydia Maria Child published this poem, originally called "A New-England Boy's Song About Thanksgiving Day," for her book *Flowers for Children, Volume 2* in 1844. The poem is based on her own memories of traveling to her grandfather's house for Thanksgiving. We have retained the punctuation and spelling of the original text for this book.

Lydia Maria Child's grandfather's house still stands near the Mystic River in Medford, Massachusetts.

For my sisters: Lauren, Melissa, and Sarah

M. T.

First edition 2011

Library of Congress Cataloging-in-Publication Data is available.
Library of Congress Catalog Card Number 2010038878
ISBN 978-0-7636-2790-4

11 12 13 14 15 16 17 CCP 10 9 8 7 6 5 4 3 2 1

Printed in Shenzhen, Guangdong, China

This book was typeset in Hadfield.
The illustrations were done in watercolor, gouache, and pencil.

Candlewick Press
99 Dover Street
Somerville, Massachusetts 02144

visit us at www.candlewick.com